Specs of Spectacle Island

A story of an island from trash to treasure

Written by Donna M. Keefe

Illustrations by Amber Leigh Luecke

Photo on back cover, Spectacle Island 1950, courtesy of Boston City Archives

Map on previous page courtesy of Boston Harbor Islands National and State Park

Published by Donna M. Keefe (June 9, 2021)

Printed in the United States

ISBN: 978-1-0879-6832-2 (pbk.)

In memory of James

*"This lump of coal has been transformed
into a beautiful diamond."*

*— former Boston mayor Tom Menino at the opening
of Spectacle Island*

Acknowledgments

A huge fan of the Big Dig, I followed the project as it evolved. When Spectacle Island opened to the public, I got on the boat. Enchanted with the history and the transformation of the island that once polluted Boston Harbor, I was inspired to write this story.

When researching images for the book, I realized a cohort of Big Dig enthusiasts remains long after any visible structure of the Central Artery was removed. I am immensely grateful to Boston Harbor Now and Dan McNichol for their support of Specs, the courageous little chipmunkel, in telling the story of Spectacle Island. A special thank you goes to the young readers, Madison and Bridget MacMillan and Trystan and Lilliana Doucette, and Amber Luecke, the talented illustrator who meticulously and patiently brought the story of Specs to life. I want to extend my boundless gratitude to my niece, Catherine Ternes, for her editorial commentary and review from the first draft of Specs of Spectacle Island to its completion.

I am forever grateful for the contributions of my family and friends and their time, encouragement, and for their endurance in letting me share my passion for the Big Dig, Spectacle Island, and my desire to tell the story of Specs. My heartfelt appreciation to everyone who played a part in helping me write this book.

I hope this story will inspire you to explore Spectacle Island and learn about its renewal. A major environmental disaster is now a beautiful and peaceful place. If you are walking one of the many trails, be sure to look for the chipmunkels.

CHAPTER ONE
The Island and the City

Who would have thought a city garbage dump heaped with trash would turn into an island gem bursting with nature? That is what happened on Spectacle Island.

Spectacle Island is one of 34 islands in Boston Harbor and just four miles from Boston, Massachusetts. It was a garbage dump for the city for close to 50 years. Toxins were leaking into Boston Harbor and polluting the water. A bulldozer once sank into a pile of trash and disappeared. The city finally closed the smelly, leaking island in 1959.

Spectacle Island has a diverse and intriguing history. It is one of the greatest stories ever told of the reclamation of land from an environmental disaster.

Native Americans used the island for fishing and clamming for thousands of years until around 1615 when European diseases killed virtually all of the native population.

Europeans began using the island in the 1630s as a source of firewood and for cattle grazing. It was later used as a smallpox quarantine. In the 1700s, ships entering the harbor were required to stop at the island where anyone showing symptoms of a contagious disease had to disembark.

In the early 1800s, the island was used exclusively for its relative remoteness from Boston. Two hotels were built in 1847, only to be closed by police ten years later. It was discovered they were being used for gambling and other illicit activities. A horse rendering plant began operating in 1857. It later became a grease extraction facility in 1903 for making soap and glycerin.

The island became the official dump for the city of Boston in 1912. It was closed in 1959 and continued to leak toxic waste into Boston Harbor until 1990. [1, 2, 3, 4, 6]

Boston was one of America's oldest cities and was established long before there were cars. The houses were built very close to each other, with their front doors sitting right at the edge of the narrow, winding streets.

Over time, the city grew and became very busy and crowded. People were now driving cars on the narrow streets and causing traffic jams. City planners needed to find a way to keep all the traffic moving through the city. More roads were needed, but there was nowhere to build them. Something had to be done. Some brilliant people came up with this fantastic idea to build an elevated road for all the cars to go above and through the middle of the city. They built a big expressway between the buildings high above the city and painted it green.

The city continued to grow with more people, more cars, and more traffic jams. Thirty years later, the big green expressway was no longer big enough. It was also falling apart. Some other brilliant people came up with another fantastic idea to tear it down and build a new expressway underground. It was to be even bigger, and all the cars would now go under the city. The best part would be all the new parks with gardens and fountains built around the city for all the people to enjoy. And the air would be cleaner, too.

Everyone agreed it was a magnificent idea. It became known as the "Big Dig," and it certainly was a big dig! It would go underneath the existing expressway through the city filled with glass-and-steel skyscrapers and a subway system running beneath it. It would be 3½ miles long, and in some places, 120 feet below the surface. There would be a tunnel where cars could travel under water and a beautiful, elegant bridge for cars to travel over water. Construction of the Big Dig began in 1991 and lasted for 16 years.

CHAPTER TWO
The Chipmunkels

Meanwhile, chipmunkels were living and thriving on Spectacle Island. They were quite happy living on the island covered with garbage. They were burrowing creatures and came above ground for spring, summer, and fall for the warm sunshine and ocean air before going back underground for the long, harsh winters.

Specs, a chipmunkel who wore glasses and had brown specks on his back, truly believed that Spectacle Island was named after him, but it wasn't. It was named Spectacle Island by European settlers. Its shape resembled a pair of eyeglasses with a narrow strip of land connecting the two mounds formed by moving glacier ice.

Specs was a rebellious chipmunkel. He never followed the rules and was always getting into trouble for not doing his chores and being late for dinner. He was inquisitive and preferred to wander and explore. He had a chunky, furry body that was quite a bit larger than the other chipmunkels his age. He started wearing glasses when he was three years old and was somewhat awkward with his slightly longer and crooked front teeth protruding from his fat little cheeks.

The other chipmunkels picked on Specs. He responded by saying his glasses let him see into the future, and one day, he would do something special. They all laughed at him. But they were jealous of how he could move through the tunnels with ease with his big, muscular body and wondered if he might be able to see into their future as well.

Along with the construction of the underground expressway, a third harbor tunnel to Logan Airport, named after the legendary Boston Red Sox baseball player Ted Williams, was also being dug.

With all the digging, a place was needed to get rid of the excavated dirt. Spectacle Island, already a trash dump, provided the perfect spot.

Close to one-third of the total amount of dirt from the Big Dig was shipped to Spectacle Island. More than 4,400 barge loads, enough dirt to fill Boston's Fenway Park twice, were dumped on the island.

A 10-lane, cable-stayed bridge, the widest ever built and the first asymmetrical hybrid design using steel and concrete was built across the Charles River. It became a landmark and gateway to Boston. [4, 7, 8]

One day a barge arrived carrying big orange and yellow tractors, trucks, and bulldozers. People in funny yellow hats kept showing up with bigger and bigger equipment. Then the bulldozing started. Boatloads of contaminated dirt were getting dumped onto the chipmunkels' home. There was constant noise. The earth was shaking and cracking.

Some of the chipmunkels got sick; some even died from the contaminated dirt. They became confused and were worried about what was happening to their island. They decided to go even farther underground. They dug deeper and deeper into the earth to escape the dumping, the noise, and the big equipment rolling over the land. It was a horrible existence, but it was the only way they knew how to survive, so they adapted to life underground.

Specs became very angry and fed up with living deep inside the earth. He refused to spend the rest of his life underground. Much to his family's dismay, he decided to leave Spectacle Island. His favorite brother Stripes cried when he heard the news. He didn't want to lose his playmate and best friend. His mother was very concerned about him leaving the island. She wanted to protect him, but she knew she had to let him go.

Specs' family and friends came up from below and stood at the shore waving good-bye. He was enormously excited about his new adventure but was also worried about what was ahead. Trying not to show his fear, he turned, smiled, and with a tear in his eye, stepped into the cold water of Boston Harbor. He swam away to explore the other islands. The chipmunkels quickly ran back to their tunnels and disappeared into the earth.

When Specs landed on George's Island, one of the harbor islands, he was not welcome. Word got out about the dirt getting dumped on Spectacle Island. He became known as the "Spectacle Creature." The inhabitants were fearful that he might contaminate their island. Every time he reached the shore, barely able to catch his breath, he was chased away.

He realized he would be better off going to a place where no one would recognize him. Thinking he might have a better chance to start over, he went to Boston. However, Specs struggled with life in the big city. He was lonely and became disappointed at how difficult it was to live there and to make friends.

For many years, Specs wandered through the neighborhoods and in and out of the subway. He was barely surviving. When it got cold, he would stay underground, where the subway trains would pass by him at rapid speeds. He knew nothing about this underground city. He was terrified by the big bright lights and harsh sounds of the squeaky wheels of the fast-moving trains.

He never expected to see so much activity underground. It was not a healthy environment for a chipmunkel. Specs was fighting to stay in the darkness that he needed to hibernate. He could not find the food he would typically eat to sustain him for the winter. He was growing weary of having to fend for himself. As he traveled through the underground city, he came upon a cave away from the bright lights. He curled up in a corner and fell asleep.

Specs was awoken by a group of boisterous mud rats who were quite angry to see him in their cave. He did not know how long he had been sleeping, but his eyes went wide when he saw the pile of garbage the mud rats had dragged into the cave. They expressed their irritation with him for intruding, but they shared their food with him.

Specs became friends with the mud rats. They taught him the tricks of navigating the underground city. They told him about the Big Dig and the tunnel being dug that was causing a lot of chaos. They also told him about the dirt that was being shipped to some island in Boston Harbor.

The mud rats weren't too happy about seeing the crusty, smelly dirt they loved being removed. To make matters worse, they had to carry their food even farther to reach the cave where they could hide. They were tired and angry because someone was always working in the tunnel day and night. They could not get any rest and started to complain. But Specs was no longer listening. At that point, he understood what was happening on Spectacle Island and knew he had to go home.

CHAPTER THREE
Specs Returns Home

On a glorious spring day, Specs arrived back home on Spectacle Island. Nothing resembled the home he left behind. He ran over the hills and into the deep valley now covered with daisies and lots of shrubs blooming with brilliant pink and white sea roses. He heard birds singing and smelled the salty air. Tall grasses swayed in the ocean breeze, and trees with bright green leaves reaching toward the sun lined the pathways. But he could not find any chipmunkels.

Construction on Spectacle Island began in 1992. The added dirt from digging the tunnel increased its size adding 60 feet to its height. At 157 feet, it is now the tallest point in the harbor.

Workers planted 2,400 trees, 26,000 shrubs, and a variety of plants and grasses to transform the island.

Spectacle Island opened to the public as a recreational area in June 2006. Visitors can enjoy hiking the five miles of trails, a swimming beach, a visitor's center with a café and museum, along with public programs and events. [2, 3, 4, 5]

Specs frantically began looking for his family. He was troubled when he could not find even one tunnel. Not being able to locate his family, he became despondent. Lonely and discouraged, he found a shady spot to rest that seemed like the place where he and Stripes would run and tumble with each other and play games. He began to cry.

But Specs wasn't giving up. While searching for his family, he encountered some unfamiliar animals who were now living on the island. They were big and small, light and dark, furry and scaly. He became fearful and wondered who they were. Feeling sorry that he ever left the island and not knowing what else he could do, he gained enough courage to approach them.

He discovered many of the strange animals were kind and wanted to help. They told him they heard about the island in Boston Harbor where they could go to make a better life. For many, it was a long journey to Spectacle Island. He listened to their stories, and like them, he had also left home in search of a better life.

He learned how they observed the giant equipment as it moved from one side of the island to the other. They kept moving to avoid being smothered with dirt or getting crushed by trucks and bulldozers. That was how they survived the confusion and the constant changes on the island.

Specs established a unique bond with Oliver, who was somewhat similar to him. Oliver traveled under the ground but did not dig deep into the earth. He moved along just slightly under the surface before popping up out of the ground. Oliver was a little eccentric and laughed a bit too loud. But Specs enjoyed his robust personality and sly grin that appeared for no reason.

Playing with Oliver reminded Specs of his brother, but no one could replace Stripes. Even though he was grateful to have a new friend, he really missed his family and the other chipmunkels.

One day Oliver took Specs to a shallow place in the valley. He told him that sometimes, on a very quiet night, he could hear faint sounds. Specs thought for a minute and then, surprising Oliver with a huge hug, exclaimed, "That's it!" His family and the other chipmunkels must have gone even farther underground.

Specs began to dig. He heard a noise and became excited. He kept digging and digging, not thinking anymore of how deep he was going. He came across a tunnel. He scurried down the tunnel and saw his brother Stripes who began squealing with delight. Stripes led Specs to their family, where they greeted him with shouts and tears of joy.

Specs was thrilled to see everyone, but he wondered why they were still living so deep underground. Their island was now a beautiful place. At that moment, he realized they had dug themselves so deep into the earth they were not aware that the digging, dumping, and noise had ended. The world had changed, and they did not know.

Specs smiled and hugged his family. He was ecstatic and anxious to share what he learned. He shouted, "Follow me!" and led them through his newly-dug tunnel to the earth above where they exited their world below.

They began laughing, dancing, and singing. Some of the other animals joined in the celebration. Specs introduced Oliver to his family, where he was warmly embraced and became an honorary chipmunkel.

Today lots of people go to Spectacle Island. Boats departing from Boston filled with visitors arrive every day. They marvel at how this magnificent little island was restored. They follow the trails up to the hilltops for spectacular views of the harbor and the Boston skyline. But more importantly, Specs is happy to be with his family again, living on Spectacle Island, the place he has always called home.

Spectacle Island is accessible by public ferry, private boats, or charter boat. The marina is located on the island's western shore.

Its hiking trails offer views of neighboring Harbor Islands and the Boston skyline. Several wooden gazebos were built to provide shade along the trails. The Krystle M. Campbell Memorial Gazebo is a tribute to one of the victims of the Boston Marathon Bombings of April 15, 2013. Krystle managed the Summer Shack and event operations on Spectacle and Georges Islands.

Spectacle Island is owned by the Massachusetts Department of Conservation and Recreation and the City of Boston. The island is part of the Boston Harbor Islands National Recreation Area, which became a National Park in 1996. [2, 3, 5, 6]

Spectacle Island

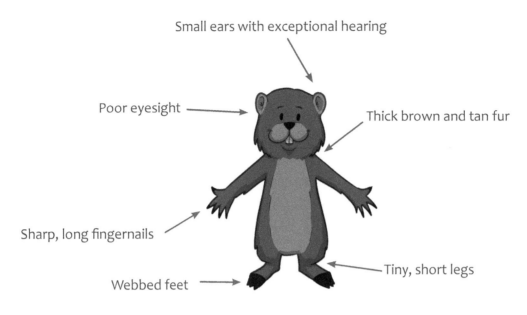

Small ears with exceptional hearing

Poor eyesight

Thick brown and tan fur

Sharp, long fingernails

Webbed feet

Tiny, short legs

DIAGRAM OF A CHIPMUNKEL

Chipmunkels are fantasy animals, which only exist on Spectacle Island. They burrow or dig deep into the earth for the winter months to stay warm and dry. Chipmunkels like to live in landfills of garbage and trash, but they cannot survive in contaminated land. During construction of the Big Dig, dirt from Boston was dumped on Spectacle Island, forcing them to go deeper underground.

Chipmunkels are fascinating creatures. They have very thick brown and tan fur, tiny short legs, and little fingers with sharp, long fingernails for digging, and webs between their fingers and toes for swimming long distances. They can hear exceptionally well with their tiny ears but cannot see very far, making it easy for them to live in tunnels. They have a very long lifespan. During the excavation of Spectacle Island, a skeleton was found and thought to be more than 50 years old.

Chipmunkels can survive for a very long time underground, eating dirt mites and creeping eels. That was how they survived living underground until the Big Dig and the restoration of Spectacle Island were completed.

ABOUT SPECTACLE ISLAND

Retrieved from: http://archive.boston.com/business/gallery/spectacleislandhistory/
https://www.bostonharborislands.org/blog/relief-and-restoration-the-big-dig/

Photos courtesy of Boston Harbor Now /Boston Harbor Cruises

- Native American tribes used the island to fish, clam, and gather food. An archaeological dig in 1992, before construction began, produced a wealth of information on Native American culture and lifestyle dating from 535 A. D. to 1590. Some artifacts reveal that Native Americans may have used the island about 8,000 years ago.

- The island got its name from early European settlers who arrived in Boston in 1630. They saw that the two large mounds connected by a sandbar in the middle of the harbor looked like a pair of spectacles. The early settlers used the island as a source of timber and for pasture land.

- In the early 1700s, the island was used as a quarantine hospital for smallpox victims. In 1847, it was home to two resort hotels that were shut down after officials discovered gambling and brothels. In 1857, a Boston businessman built a horse-rendering factory that processed as many as 2,000 horses a year into glue stock, hair, oil, and bones. It later became a grease extraction facility in 1903 for making soap and glycerin.

- Boston used Spectacle Island as a dump for the city from 1912- 1959. The landfill was closed in 1959 after a bulldozer disappeared into a heap of trash. It remained an eyesore and public health hazard leaking toxins into Boston Harbor.

- Working together, the City of Boston, the Department of Environmental Management, and the Massachusetts Department of Environmental Protection came up with a plan to solve the environmental nightmare. Spectacle Island provided a place to put the excavated material from the Big Dig (Central Artery/Tunnel Project) and build a new park.

- Construction on Spectacle Island began in 1993. Dirt and gravel were used to reshape the island. It was capped with two feet of clay and covered with two to five feet of topsoil placed above the cap for planting trees and other vegetation. Workers planted 2,400 trees and 26,000 shrubs in the fresh soil. The island joined the national parks system in 1996 and opened for visitors in June 2006.

- The island's environmentally friendly systems include composting toilets with no water or chemicals, electric vehicles, and water from the sinks is filtered and used to water the plants. The visitor center, powered by solar panels, is graced with Adirondack chairs lining the front porch overlooking the harbor with views of the Boston skyline.

"Most people remember the Big Dig as a big headache, but there is a story of success here – from trash to treasure."

—Tiffany Dumont, park ranger

"Only two years ago it was nothing more than a mountain of garbage in the middle of Boston Harbor, leaking thousands of gallons of toxic material into the surrounding water."

—Peter Zuk, former CA/T Project Director

Photos courtesy of Boston Harbor Now /Boston Harbor Cruises

ABOUT THE BIG DIG

Retrieved from: https://www.washingtonpost.com/wp-dyn/content/article/2007/12/25/AR2007122500600.html

When the clock runs out on 2007, Boston will quietly mark the end of one of the most tumultuous eras in the city's history: The Big Dig, the nation's most complex and costliest highway project, will officially come to an end. The joint venture teamed megaproject contractor Bechtel/Parsons Brinckerhoff with the Massachusetts Turnpike Authority to build the dizzying array of underground highways, bridges, ramps, and a new tunnel under Boston Harbor -- all while the city remained open for business.

Image: Northeastern University Library

Of all the project's Rubik's Cube-like engineering challenges, none was more daunting than the first -- how to build a wider tunnel directly underneath a narrower existing elevated highway while preventing the overhead highway from collapsing.

To solve the problem, engineers created horizontal braces as wide as the new tunnel, then cut away the elevated highway's original metal struts and gently lowered them onto the braces -- even as cars crawled along overhead, their drivers oblivious to the work below.

The Big Dig would have to undertake the massive project in the cramped confines of Boston's narrow, winding streets, some dating to pre-Colonial days. For those who grew up with the noise and clutter of the old Central Artery, the transformation of downtown Boston is still a wonder to behold. The dark parking lots under the old elevated highway have been replaced by a park, dubbed the Rose Fitzgerald Kennedy Greenway. Buildings that turned their backs to the old Central Artery are finding ways to open their doors to the parkway.

"It was always a beautiful city, but it had this ugly scar through it," said Salvucci, the force behind the project and state transportation secretary during the project's planning stages. Rather than build a new elevated highway, Salvucci and others pushed a far more radical solution: burying it. "The Big Dig is not a highway with an incidental city adjacent to it. It is a living city that happens to have some major highway infrastructure within it, and that highway infrastructure had to be rebuilt," he said. "This was not elective surgery. It had to be done."

BACKGROUND OF THE BIG DIG
CENTRAL ARTERY/TUNNEL PROJECT
Retrieved from: https://www.mass.gov/info-details/the-big-dig-project-background

THE PROBLEM

Boston, Massachusetts, had a world-class traffic problem, an elevated six-lane highway called the Central Artery that ran through the center of downtown. When it opened in 1959, the Central Artery carried about 75,000 vehicles a day. It has carried upwards of 200,000 making it one of the most congested highways in the United States. Traffic crawled for more than 10 hours each day. Without major improvements to the Central Artery and the harbor crossings, Boston expected a stop-and-go traffic jam for up to 16 hours a day - every waking hour - by 2010. Traffic wasn't the only problem the old Central Artery caused in Boston. The elevated highway, which displaced 20,000 residents, also cut off Boston's North End and Waterfront neighborhoods from the downtown, limiting their participation in the city's economic life.

THE SOLUTION

The project had two major components. One was replacing the six-lane elevated highway with an eight-to-ten-lane underground expressway directly beneath the existing road culminating at the northern point with a 14-lane, two-bridge crossing over the Charles River. The other was the extension of I-90, the Massachusetts Turnpike, from south of downtown Boston with a tunnel beneath South Boston and the Boston Harbor to Logan Airport. The first link of the connection, the four-lane Ted Williams Tunnel under the harbor, completed the 3,089 miles of Interstate 90 from Boston to Seattle, WA.

THE CHALLENGES

The Central Artery/Tunnel Project became known as the Big Dig. It is public works on a scale comparable to some of the great projects of the last century, the Panama Canal, the English Channel Tunnel (the "Chunnel"), and the Trans-Alaska Pipeline. Each of these projects presented unique challenges.

Photo courtesy of Boston City Archives

The Central Artery/Tunnel Project's unique challenge was to construct the roadway in the middle of Boston without crippling the city. The work of the project and its magnitude and duration had never been attempted in the heart of an urban area. Unlike any other major highway project, it was designed to maintain traffic capacity and access to residents and businesses, keeping the city open for business throughout construction.

Building an expressway underground in a city like Boston proved to be one of the largest, most technically difficult, and environmentally challenging infrastructure projects ever undertaken in the United States. The project's 7.8 miles of highway had close to 50 separate designs divided into 118 separate construction contracts, with 26 geotechnical drilling contracts. At the peak of construction, 5,000 construction workers were on the project, and workers did about $3 million of work each day.

Photo courtesy of Boston City Archives

About 150 cranes were in use project-wide. The deepest point is 120 feet and runs beneath the Red Line subway tunnel at Dewey Square. The highest point is at State Street, where the highway passes over the Blue Line subway tunnel, and the roof of the highway is the street above. The larger of the two Charles River bridges, a ten-lane cable-stayed hybrid bridge, is the widest ever built and the first to use an asymmetrical design. It was named the Leonard P. Zakim Bunker Hill Memorial Bridge.

GOALS AND ACHIEVEMENTS

Along with improved mobility in a notoriously congested city, the Central Artery/Tunnel Project reconnected neighborhoods severed by the old elevated highway and improved the quality of life in the city. Boston's carbon monoxide levels dropped 12 percent citywide. The Big Dig was an engineering feat like no other. It made significant advances in roadway construction and urban planning. It created more than 300 acres of new parks and open space, including the 27 acres of the Rose Kennedy Greenway, more than 100 acres on Spectacle Island where dirt from the project capped the abandoned dump, and 40 acres along the Charles River.

ABOUT THE LEONARD P. ZAKIM BUNKER HILL MEMORIAL BRIDGE

THE ZAKIM

Retreived from: https://leonardpzakimbunkerhillbridge.org/
https://www.bostonglobe.com/metro/2012/08/08/bright-idea-brings-new-lights-zakim-bridge/svX9qD6ys-D3Ks2vH1iU1eO/story.html

> *"We honor his memory, not by this beautiful bridge... but by continuing on in his fight for social justice."*
>
> —Bruce Springsteen at the opening day of the Zakim Bridge

The Leonard P. Zakim Bunker Hill Memorial Bridge, affectionately called The Zakim, is the world's widest cable-stayed bridge. It is named after civil rights activist Lenny Zakim who championed "building bridges between peoples" and the American colonists who fought the British in the Battle of Bunker Hill. It has become a landmark of Boston.

> *"Lenny lived by the belief that each of us has a moral responsibility to make the world a better, more inclusive and respectful place for all people. He worked tirelessly to build personal bridges between our city's diverse people and neighborhoods. He would be so proud to know that this magnificent structure will stand as a symbol of unity, hope, and respect for all Bostonians."*
>
> —Joyce Zakim, wife of activist Lenny Zakim
>
> at the 2002 bridge dedication

BACKGROUND

The two 270 foot towers of the cable-stayed bridge across the Charles River link the past and future of Boston. The inverted Y-shaped towers reflect the shape of the Bunker Hill Monument in Charlestown, which marks the location of one of the first major battles of the American Revolution. The cables extending from the two towers form massive triangles, emulating the appearance of ships' sails as a reminder of Boston as a shipbuilding center throughout American history. They are a tribute to the USS Constitution, a leading ship of the War of 1812 and built in Boston Harbor.

The Swiss civil engineer Christian Menn developed the concept for the bridge. The design was engineered by American civil engineer Ruchu Hsu with Bechtel Parson Brinckerhoff. At 1,432 feet long, it emerges from the underground Central Artery. Large diamond-shaped holes were cut into the deck to allow daylight to filter down to the water below. The holes were integrated into the design so the alewife fish migrating up the river would not lose their way in the shadows created by the bridge.

One night the bridge could be blue, then green for the Celtics, then gold for the Bruins, or any combination of colors to mark different philanthropic events. "Lenny would love these new lights," she said. "It will light up for different causes, and he was all about reaching out to different communities."

In an interview with *The Boston Globe*, bridge architect Miguel Rosales said, "The bridge is supposed to have the feel of a regal entry to Boston, the towers bathed in blue, the cables highlighted in gleaming white." Lit with bright blue light, the Zakim Bridge is an instantly recognizable feature of the city skyline.

Photo courtesy of City of Boston

ABOUT THE ROSE FITZGERALD KENNEDY GREENWAY

Retrieved from: https://tclf.org/rose-fitzgerald-kennedy-greenway?destination=search-results

Winding through downtown Boston, this 1.5-mile linear series of parks and open spaces measures seventeen acres along the path of a former elevated highway. The Greenway is the result of the decades-long Central Artery Project, which buried Interstate 93.

The Rose Fitzgerald Kennedy Greenway is named after Rose Kennedy, who grew up in the North End and mother of Sen. Edward M. Kennedy. The project and its distinct parks restored visual and physical connectivity between downtown Boston and several historic neighborhoods, including the North End, Long Wharf, South Station, and Chinatown. The parks that make up The Greenway are unique in character and spatial composition. They include Chinatown Park, Dewey Square, Fort Point Channel Parks, Wharf District Parks, Armenian Heritage Park, and North End Parks.

THE GREENWAY

Retrieved from: https://www.rosekennedygreenway.org/history/

The Greenway is the contemporary public park in the heart of Boston. In 1991, after almost a decade of planning, construction began in Boston on the Central Artery/Tunnel Project, more widely known as the "Big Dig." The project, recognized as one of the largest, most complex, and technologically challenging in the history of the United States, would remove the elevated highway and create a tunnel system below the city.

With the elevated highway relocated underground, community and political leaders seized the opportunity to enhance the city by creating The Greenway, a public park that reconnected some of Boston's oldest and most vibrant neighborhoods and the city itself with the waterfront. The creation of The Greenway was a joint effort of the Massachusetts Turnpike Authority (since incorporated into the Massachusetts Department of Transportation), the Commonwealth of Massachusetts, the City of Boston, and various civic and community organizations.

The Greenway Conservancy, an independently incorporated non-profit organization, was established in 2004. In 2008, the State Legislature confirmed the Conservancy as the designated steward of The Greenway. It opened to the public in October of 2008 with tens of thousands of visitors coming together for the park's inaugural celebration. In 2009, the Greenway Conservancy assumed operational responsibility for the park.

Photo credit: Kyle Klein Photography, courtesy of the Greenway Conservancy

NOTES

1. "Spectacle Island," Friends of the Boston Harbor Islands, Established 1979, accessed January 10, 2021, http://www.fbhi.org/spectacle-island.html.

2. "Spectacle Island," Spectacle Island | The Cultural Landscape Foundation, accessed January 10, 2021, https://tclf.org/spectacle-island.

3. *"Exploring Spectacle Island. A Self-guided Tour."* (Boston Harbor Islands, n.d.).

4. "The Evolution of Spectacle Island," Boston.com (The Boston Globe), accessed January 10, 2021, http://archive.boston.com/business/gallery/spectacleislandhistory//.

5. "Spectacle Island (Massachusetts)," Wikipedia (Wikimedia Foundation, January 10, 2021), https://en.wikipedia.org/wiki/Spectacle_Island_(Massachusetts).

6. "Spectacle Island," Boston Harbor Islands, accessed February 13, 2021, https://www.bostonharborislands.org/spectacle-island/.

7. "Verdict Media Limited," Verdict Traffic, accessed January 10, 2021, https://www.roadtraffic-technology.com/projects/big_dig/.

8. "The Big Dig: Project Background," Mass.gov, accessed January 10, 2021, https://www.mass.gov/info-details/the-big-dig-project-background.

RESOURCES

Bilis, Madeline. "TBT: When Spectacle Island Was a Heaping Pile of Trash," Boston Magazine, May 5, 2016, accessed January 10, 2021, https://www.bostonmagazine.com/news/2016/05/05/spectacle-island-trash/.

Boston Harbor Islands National Recreation Area | SPECTACLE ISLAND, National Park Planner, accessed February 18, 2021, https://npplan.com/parks-by-state/massachusetts-national-parks/boston-harbor-islands-national-recreation-area-park-at-a-glance/boston-harbor-islands-national-recreation-area-spectacle-island/.

Flint, Anthony. "10 years later, did the Big Dig deliver? The $15 billion project is a road paved with failures, successes, and what-if," The Boston Globe, December 29, 2015, accessed January 10, 2021, https://www.bostonglobe.com/magazine/2015/12/29/years-later-did-big-dig-deliver/tSb8PIMS4Q-JUETsMpA7SpI/story.html?event=event12.

The Greenway, The Rose Kennedy Greenway, accessed February 13, 2021, https://www.rosekennedygreenway.org/history/.

Klein, Christopher. "A harbor Spectacle," The Boston Globe, June 22, 2008, accessed February 23, 2021, http://archive.boston.com/travel/boston/articles/2008/06/22/a_harbor_spectacle/?page=1.

LeBlanc, Steve. "On December 31, It's Official: Boston's Big Dig Will Be Done," The Washington Post, WP Company, December 26, 2007, accessed January 10, 2021, http://washingtonpost.com/wp-dyn/content/article/2007/12/25/AR2007122500600.html?nav=hcmoduletmv.

The Lenny Zakim Fund, accessed February 18, 2012, https://thelennyzakimfund.org/.

Leonard P. Zakim Bunker Hill Memorial Bridge, November 25, 2020, accessed January 10, 2021, https://leonardpzakimbunkerhillbridge.org/.

McNichol, Dan. *The Big Dig Trivia Quiz Book.* New York: Silver Lining Books, 2002.

McNichol, Dan. *The Big Dig.* New York: Silver Lining Books, 2000.

"Spectacle Island Remediation/Land Reclamation," accessed January 10, 2021, https://www.jaycashman.com/work/spectacle-island-remediation-land-reclamation-boston-harbor/.

Study.com, accessed March 22, 2021, https://study.com/academy/lesson/zakim-bridge-construction-facts.html.

"Tour of the Projects-The Big Dig," PBS, accessed March 22, 2021, https://www.pbs.org/greatprojects/tour/bigdig_5.html.

CPSIA information can be obtained
at www.ICGtesting.com
Printed in the USA
BVHW021007100621
609275BV00008B/1773